To Noa, Maya, and Serena

-D.T.

Babbit & Joan,
a Rabbit and a Phone

written and illustrated by

Denise Turu

flyaway
books

It all began when the phones went on strike.

Babbit the rabbit watched from his window.
He had never thought about how hard the phones worked.

He went to check on his own phone, Joan.
She was exhausted! She'd been taking pictures
and sending texts for Babbit all day, every day.

That afternoon, Babbit tucked Joan in for a nap.
"Rest well, my friend!" he said.

Then he took a deep breath and stepped
outside, leaving Joan behind.

For the first time ever, Babbit felt alone.
His neighbors were very busy, and no one
said hello. What should he do?

Babbit decided to go for a walk.
When he reached the forest, he kept going.
He'd never been so far on his own before.

Soon he saw a mother snail
carrying her baby on her back.
He'd never seen that before.

Then he found a beautiful exotic plant.
He'd never seen that before either.

Later he came across ants carrying
leaves ten times their size.
There were so many surprises
in the forest!

Babbit walked and walked and looked and looked—
and then he realized he was lost. Without Joan,
how would he find his way back?

Babbit tried to remember which way
he had come. Just as he was getting
really worried, he heard a chirpy melody.

It was a little blue bird. "I was headed to the city to give a concert at the Eagle Square," he said. "But now I'm lost, and my phone is out of batteries!" His name was Ed.

A moment later, **Babbit** and **Ed**
heard a growling sound
from behind the trees.

It was a big brown bear. "I was going to visit my brother in the city, but now I can't find my way," she cried. "I lost my phone when I went swimming in the river!" Her name was Mair.

"Let's stay together," said Babbit. The three friends
walked on and on, in search of a way back to the city.

The colors of the forest began to change
as the sun began to set.

As it grew dark, they found a place
to sleep. There they told stories
and laughed together around the bonfire.

Long into the night, Babbit lay awake
and gazed up at the sky. He had never seen
the moon and stars shine so brightly before.

The next morning, the friends continued their journey, ready to see new things and find their way home. They were amazed when they found a grove of tropical palm trees.

Up in the treetops, the toucan family, so colorful and noisy, was even more amazing.

Ed flew higher and chirped his loudest.
"Which way to the city, friends?"
"That way! That way!" the toucans called.

Babbit, Ed, and Mair walked
until they reached the river, where they found
an old wooden boat—and a clue.

Mair was the strongest, so she rowed. Ed had a beautiful voice,
so he sang. And Babbit, whose eyesight was the best,
guided them on their way.

As the sun rose higher, they saw the city ahead.

"What an adventure!" said Babbit. "Good-bye for now!" Mair said.
Ed hummed a farewell tune to his new friends.
They all promised to meet again soon.

His neighborhood looked the same, but Babbit felt different. No one had noticed he had gone, and no one noticed he was back.

But Joan did. Babbit was happy to see
that she was feeling better. He told her about
his new friends and all that he had discovered.

They made a deal. Joan would take more breaks
to recharge her batteries. And sometimes Babbit
would go out on his own to explore the world.

That night, Babbit tucked Joan into her own little bed. Then they slept peacefully, getting ready for a new day.

The End